Quentin Blake

ANGELICA SPROCKET'S POCKETS

RED FOX

For l'équipe QB,
with love and thanks

Angelica Sprocket lives next door.
Her overcoat has pockets galore.

There's a pocket
for mice,

and a pocket
for cheese

and a pocket for hankies
in case anyone feels that they're
going to sneeze.

There's a pocket for all kinds of umbrellas

for when it begins to rain.

And another one with
swimming costumes and towels

for when the sun
comes out again.

There's a pocket for ducks,
and a pocket
for boats

and a pocket with lovely straw hats

for GOATS.

And in case anyone is thinking
of dropping off to sleep,
there's a pocket for

motorhorns that go PAH-HEE-

HAR-HUR and BEEP-BEEP.

There's a pocket for skateboards
(just look at those
skaters!)

and another pocket for

ALLIGATORS.

There's a pocket for ice cream
and all kinds of nice things
to drink.

There's a pocket for
　　saucepans and frying pans and buckets

and spoons and forks and cheesegraters and

the kitchen SINK.

There's a

pocket for an

ELEPHANT, green and pink,

and another pocket for...

WHAT DO
YOU THINK?

There's more and more
and more
and more.
Angelica Sprocket has pockets galore!

RED FOX
UK | USA | Canada | Ireland | Australia
India | New Zealand | South Africa

Red Fox is part of the Penguin Random House group of companies
whose addresses can be found at global.penguinrandomhouse.com.

www.penguin.co.uk   www.puffin.co.uk   www.ladybird.co.uk

Penguin
Random House
UK

First published by Jonathan Cape 2010
Red Fox edition published 2011
This edition published 2018
001

Made and printed in China
A CIP catalogue record for this book is available from the British Library

ISBN: 978–1–782–95862–8

All correspondence to:
Red Fox, Penguin Random House Children's
80 Strand, London WC2R 0RL

MIX
Paper from
responsible sources
FSC® C018179